PAPERBACK P

Contents

John Reynolds Gardiner

is a writer with a great enthusiasm for sharing his craft. He visits elementary schools regularly to offer his advice about writing to young writers. *Stone Fox,* his first book to be published, has sold over one million copies. It has been translated into four languages and made into a movie for television.

Marcia Sewall

has been influenced by her creative parents: Her mother was an artist and her father a storyteller. "I do love to translate words into pictures," she says. "I love to draw out of my imagination people and places." Ms. Sewell has illustrated many books for children. She lives and works in Boston.

STONE FOX

STONE FOX

by John Reynolds Gardiner

Illustrated by Marcia Sewall

HOUGHTON MIFFLIN COMPANY

BOSTON

ATLANTA   DALLAS   GENEVA, ILLINOIS   PALO ALTO   PRINCETON

Author's Acknowledgments

I would like to pay credit to Andrew J. Galambos for the many ideas and concepts of his, based on his theory of primary property and the science of volition, that appear in this book.

I would like to express my sincere gratitude to Martin Tahse, without whom this book would not have been written. I am also grateful to Barbara Fenton, my editor, for her solicitous guidance and contribution; Ken Gardiner, my brother, for inspiring me to become a writer; Sylvia Hirsch, my agent, for encouraging me through the years; and Gloria, my wife, for providing the tranquility every writer dreams of.

Acknowledgments

Grateful acknowledgment is made for use of the following material:

Text

1 *Stone Fox,* by John Reynolds Gardiner, illustrated by Marcia Sewall. Text copyright © 1980 by John Reynolds Gardiner. Illustrations copyright © 1980 by Marcia Sewall. Reprinted by permission of HarperCollins Publishers. **84** "Race Days," from January 1992 *Ranger Rick* magazine. Copyright © 1992 by The National Wildlife Federation. Reprinted by permission. **90** "Mighty Mushing Machine," originally, "Going Sledding," by Layne Cameron, from December 1993 *U*S* Kids* magazine. Copyright © 1993 by Children's Better Health Institute, Benjamin Franklin Literary & Medical, Inc., Indianapolis, IN. Reprinted by permission. **94** "A Doggone Champion: Susan Butcher," by Layne Cameron, from February/March 1994 *Child Life* magazine. Copyright © 1994 by Children's Better Health Institute, Benjamin Franklin Literary & Medical, Inc., Indianapolis, IN. Reprinted by permission.

Photography

ii Courtesy of John Reynolds Gardiner (tl); Kindra Clineff (br). **84** John W. Warden (t); Skip Moody (cover). **85** John W. Warden. **87** John W. Warden. **89** John W. Warden. **90** Kevin Foster (cover). **90–91** Kent Dannen. **94** Jeff Schultz/Alaska Stock Images (t); Jeff Schultz/Alaska Stock Images (cover). **95** Jeff Schultz/Alaska Stock Images. **96** Jeff Schultz/Alaska Stock Images (t). **96–97** Jeff Schultz/Alaska Stock Images (b). **98** Reull Griffin Collection in the Archives, Alaska and Polar Regions Department, University of Alaska Fairbanks (tr); Tom Saylor (bl); Tony Scarpetta (br). **98–99** Tony Scarpetta (c). **99** Bob Winsett (t); Mark Jespersen/Animals Magazine (c); David Allen (b). **100** Tracey Wheeler. **101** Courtesy of The Moody Family Archives. **102** Courtesy of The Moody Family Archives (c); Tracey Wheeler (signature, b).

1997 Impression
Houghton Mifflin Edition, 1996
Copyright © 1996 by Houghton Mifflin Company. All rights reserved.

Printed in the U.S.A.

ISBN 0-395-73247-6

6789-HC-98 97 96

To Bob at Hudson's Café

Contents

STONE FOX

1

Grandfather

One day Grandfather wouldn't get out of bed. He just lay there and stared at the ceiling and looked sad.

At first little Willy thought he was playing.

Little Willy lived with his grandfather on a small potato farm in Wyoming. It was hard work living on a potato farm, but it was also a lot of fun. Especially when Grandfather felt like playing.

Like the time Grandfather dressed up as the scarecrow out in the garden. It took little Willy an hour to catch on. Boy, did they laugh. Grandfather laughed so hard he cried. And when he cried his beard filled up with tears.

Grandfather always got up real early in the morning. So early that it was still dark outside. He would make a fire. Then he would make breakfast and call little Willy. "Hurry up or you'll be eating with the chickens," he would say. Then he would throw his head back and laugh.

Once little Willy went back to sleep. When he woke up, he found his plate out in the chicken coop. It was picked clean. He never slept late again after that.

That is . . . until this morning. For some reason Grandfather had forgotten to call him. That's when little Willy discovered that Grandfather was still in bed. There could be only one explanation. Grandfather was playing. It was another trick.

Or was it?

"Get up, Grandfather," little Willy said. "I don't want to play anymore."

But Grandfather didn't answer.

Little Willy ran out of the house.

· *Grandfather* ·

A dog was sleeping on the front porch. "Come on, Searchlight!" little Willy cried out. The dog jumped to its feet and together they ran off down the road.

Searchlight was a big black dog. She had a white spot on her forehead the size of a silver dollar. She was an old dog—actually born on the same day as little Willy, which was over ten years ago.

A mile down the road they came to a small log cabin surrounded by tall trees. Doc Smith was sitting in a rocking chair under one of the trees, reading a book.

"Doc Smith," little Willy called out. He was out of breath. "Come quick."

"What seems to be the matter, Willy?" the doctor asked, continuing to read.

Doc Smith had snow white hair and wore a long black dress. Her skin was tan and her face was covered with wrinkles.

"Grandfather won't answer me," little Willy said.

"Probably just another trick," Doc Smith replied. "Nothing to worry about."

"But he's still in bed."

Doc Smith turned a page and continued to read. "How late did you two stay up last night?"

"We went to bed early, real early. No singing or music or anything."

Doc Smith stopped reading.

· *Grandfather* ·

"Your grandfather went to bed without playing his harmonica?" she asked.

Little Willy nodded.

Doc Smith shut her book and stood up. "Hitch up Rex for me, Willy," she said. "I'll get my bag."

Rex was Doc Smith's horse. He was a handsome palomino. Little Willy hitched Rex to the wagon, and then they rode back to Grandfather's farm. Searchlight ran on ahead, leading the way and barking. Searchlight enjoyed a good run.

Grandfather was just the same. He hadn't moved.

Searchlight put her big front paws up on the bed and rested her head on Grandfather's chest. She licked his beard, which was full of tears.

Doc Smith proceeded to examine Grandfather. She used just about everything in her little black bag.

"What's that for?" little Willy asked. "What are you doing now?"

"Must you ask so many questions?" Doc Smith said.

"Grandfather says it's good to ask questions."

Doc Smith pulled a long silver object from her doctor's bag.

"What's that for?" little Willy asked.

"Hush!"

"Yes, ma'am. I'm sorry."

When Doc Smith had finished her examination, she put everything back into her little black bag. Then she walked over to the window and looked out at the field of potatoes.

After a moment she asked, "How's the crop this year, Willy?"

"Grandfather says it's the best ever."

Doc Smith rubbed her wrinkled face.

"What's wrong with him?" little Willy asked.

"Do you owe anybody money?" she asked.

"No!" little Willy answered. "What's wrong? Why won't you tell me what's wrong?"

9

"That's just it," she said. "There is *nothing* wrong with him."

"You mean he's not sick?"

"Medically, he's as healthy as an ox. Could live to be a hundred if he wanted to."

"I don't understand," little Willy said.

Doc Smith took a deep breath. And then she began, "It happens when a person gives up. Gives up on life. For whatever reason. Starts up here in the mind first; then it spreads to the body. It's a real sickness, all right. And there's no cure except in the person's own mind. I'm sorry, child, but it appears that your grandfather just doesn't want to live anymore."

Little Willy was silent for a long time before he spoke. "But what about . . . fishing . . . and the Rodeo . . . and turkey dinners? Doesn't he want to do those things anymore?"

Grandfather shut his eyes and tears rolled down his cheeks and disappeared into his beard.

"I'm sure he does," Doc Smith said, putting her

arm around little Willy. "It must be something else."

Little Willy stared at the floor. "I'll find out. I'll find out what's wrong and make it better. You'll see. I'll make Grandfather want to live again."

And Searchlight barked loudly.

2

Little Willy

A ten-year-old boy cannot run a farm. But you can't tell a ten-year-old boy that. Especially a boy like little Willy.

Grandfather grew potatoes, and that's exactly what little Willy was going to do.

The harvest was just weeks away, and little Willy was sure that if the crop was a good one, Grandfather would get well. Hadn't Grandfather been overly concerned about the crop this year? Hadn't he insisted that every square inch of land be planted? Hadn't he gotten up in the middle of the night to check the irrigation? "Gonna be our best ever, Willy," he had said. And he had said it over and over again.

Yes, after the harvest, everything would be all right. Little Willy was sure of it.

But Doc Smith wasn't.

"He's getting worse," she said three weeks later. "It's best to face these things, Willy. Your grandfather is going to die."

"He'll get better. You'll see. Wait till after the harvest."

Doc Smith shook her head. "I think you should consider letting Mrs. Peacock in town take care of him, like she does those other sickly folks. He'll be in good hands until the end comes." Doc Smith stepped up into the wagon. "You can come live with me until we make plans." She looked at Searchlight. "I'm sure there's a farmer in these parts who needs a good work dog."

Searchlight growled, causing Doc Smith's horse, Rex, to pull the wagon forward a few feet.

"Believe me, Willy, it's better this way."

13

"No!" shouted little Willy. "We're a family, don't you see? We gotta stick together!"

Searchlight barked loudly, causing the horse to rear up on his hind legs and then take off running. Doc Smith jammed her foot on the brake, but it didn't do any good. The wagon disappeared down the road in a cloud of dust.

Little Willy and Searchlight looked at each other and then little Willy broke out laughing. Searchlight joined him by barking again.

Little Willy knelt down, took Searchlight by the ears, and looked directly into her eyes. She had the greenest eyes you've ever seen. "I won't ever give you away. Ever. I promise." He put his arms around the dog's strong neck and held her tightly. "I love you, Searchlight." And Searchlight understood, for she had heard those words many times before.

That evening little Willy made a discovery.

He was sitting at the foot of Grandfather's bed playing the harmonica. He wasn't as good as

· *Little Willy* ·

Grandfather by a long shot, and whenever he missed a note Searchlight would put her head back and howl.

Once, when little Willy was way off key, Searchlight actually grabbed the harmonica in her mouth and ran out of the room with it.

"Do you want me to play some more?" little Willy asked Grandfather, knowing very well that Grandfather would not answer. Grandfather had not talked—not one word—for over three weeks.

But something happened that was almost like talking.

Grandfather put his hand down on the bed with his palm facing upward. Little Willy looked at the hand for a long time and then asked, in a whisper, "Does that mean 'yes'?"

Grandfather closed his hand slowly, and then opened it again.

Little Willy rushed to the side of the bed. His eyes were wild with excitement. "What's the sign for 'no'?"

Grandfather turned his hand over and laid it flat on the bed. Palm down meant "no." Palm up meant "yes."

Before the night was over they had worked out other signals in their hand-and-finger code. One finger meant "I'm hungry." Two fingers meant "water." But most of the time little Willy just asked questions that Grandfather could answer either "yes" or "no."

And Searchlight seemed to know what was going on, for she would lick Grandfather's hand every time he made a sign.

The next day little Willy began to prepare for the harvest.

There was a lot of work to be done. The underground shed—where the potatoes would be stored until they could be sold—had to be cleaned. The potato sacks had to be inspected, and mended if need be. The plow had to be sharpened. But most important, because Grandfather's old mare had

died last winter, a horse to pull the plow had to be
located and rented.

It was going to be difficult to find a horse, because most farmers were not interested in over-
working their animals—for any price.

Grandfather kept his money in a strongbox
under the boards in the corner of his bedroom.
Little Willy got the box out and opened it. It was
empty! Except for some letters that little Willy
didn't bother to read.

There was no money to rent a horse.

No money for anything else, for that matter.
Little Willy had had no idea they were broke. Everything they had needed since Grandfather took
sick little Willy had gotten at Lester's General
Store on credit against this year's crop.

No wonder Grandfather was so concerned. No
wonder he had gotten sick.

Little Willy had to think of something. And
quick.

17

It was now the middle of September. The potatoes they had planted in early June took from ninety to one hundred twenty days to mature, which meant they must be harvested soon. Besides, the longer he waited, the more danger there was that an early freeze would destroy the crop. And little Willy was sure that if the crop died, Grandfather would die too.

A friend of Grandfather's offered to help, but little Willy said no. "Don't accept help unless you can pay for it," Grandfather had always said. "Especially from friends."

And then little Willy remembered something.

His college money! He had enough to rent a horse, pay for help, everything. He told Grandfather about his plan, but Grandfather signaled "no." Little Willy pleaded with him. But Grandfather just repeated "no, no, no!"

The situation appeared hopeless.

But little Willy was determined. He would dig up the potatoes by hand if he had to.

· *Little Willy* ·

And then Searchlight solved the problem.

She walked over and stood in front of the plow. In her mouth was the harness she wore during the winter when she pulled the snow sled.

Little Willy shook his head. "Digging up a field is not the same as riding over snow," he told her. But Searchlight just stood there and would not move. "You don't have the strength, girl." Little Willy tried to talk her out of it. But Searchlight had made up her mind.

The potato plant grows about two feet high, but there are no potatoes on it. The potatoes are all underground. The plow digs up the plants and churns the potatoes to the surface, where they can be picked up and put into sacks.

It took little Willy and Searchlight over ten days to complete the harvest. But they made it! Either the dirt was softer than little Willy had thought, or Searchlight was stronger, because she actually seemed to enjoy herself.

And the harvest was a big one—close to two

hundred bushels per acre. And each bushel weighed around sixty pounds.

Little Willy inspected the potatoes, threw out the bad ones, and put the rest into sacks. He then put the sacks into the underground shed.

Mr. Leeks, a tall man with a thin face, riding a horse that was also tall and had a thin face, came out to the farm and bought the potatoes. Last year Grandfather had sold the crop to Mr. Leeks, so that's what little Willy did this year.

"We made it, Grandfather," little Willy said, as tears of happiness rolled down his cheeks. "See?" Little Willy held up two handfuls of money. "You can stop worrying. You can get better now."

Grandfather put his hand down on the bed. Palm down meant "no." It was not the crop he'd been worried about. It was something else. Little Willy had been wrong all along.

3

Searchlight

It's easy to tell when it's winter in Wyoming. There is snow on everything: the trees, the houses, the roads, the fields, and even the people, if they stay outside long enough.

It's not a dirty snow. It's a clean, soft snow that rests like a blanket over the entire state. The air is clear and crisp, and the rivers are all frozen. It's fun to be outdoors and see the snowflakes float down past the brim of your hat, and hear the squeak of the fresh powder under your boots.

Winter in Wyoming can be the most beautiful time of the year . . . if you're ready for it.

Little Willy was ready.

He had chopped enough wood. They would not be cold. He had stocked enough food. They would not go hungry. He had asked Lester at the general store how much food Grandfather had bought last year. Then he had purchased the same amount. This would be more than enough, because Grandfather wasn't eating very much these days.

The coming of snow, as early as October, also meant the coming of school. But little Willy didn't mind. He liked school. However, his teacher, Miss Williams, had told Grandfather once, "Far as I'm concerned, that boy of yours just asks too many questions." Grandfather had just laughed and said, "How's he gonna learn if he don't ask?"

Then, later, Grandfather had said to little Willy, "If your teacher don't know—you ask me. If I don't know—you ask the library. If the library don't know—then you've really got yourself a good question!"

Grandfather had taught little Willy a lot. But

now little Willy was on his own.

Each morning he would get up and make a fire. Then he would make oatmeal mush for breakfast. He ate it. Searchlight ate it. Grandfather ate it. He would feed Grandfather a spoonful at a time.

After breakfast little Willy would hitch up Searchlight to the sled. It was an old wooden sled that Grandfather had bought from the Indians. It was so light that little Willy could pick it up with one hand. But it was strong and sturdy.

Little Willy rode on the sled standing up and Searchlight would pull him five miles across the snow-covered countryside to the schoolhouse, which was located on the outskirts of town.

Searchlight loved the snow. She would wait patiently outside the schoolhouse all day long. And little Willy never missed a chance to run out between classes and play with his friend.

After school, they would go into the town of Jackson and run errands. They would pick up supplies at Lester's General Store, or go to the post

office, or go to the bank.

Little Willy had fifty dollars in a savings account at the bank. Every month Grandfather had deposited the money little Willy had earned working on the farm. "Don't thank me," Grandfather would say. "You earned it. You're a good little worker and I'm proud of you."

Grandfather wanted little Willy to go to college and become educated. All little Willy wanted to do was grow potatoes, but he respected his grandfather enough to do whatever he said.

If there were no errands to run that day, Searchlight would just pull little Willy up and down Main Street. Little Willy loved to look at all the people, especially the "city slickers," as Grandfather called them. Why, they didn't know a potato from a peanut, Grandfather said, and their hands were as pink and soft as a baby's. You couldn't miss the city slickers. They were the ones who looked as if they were going to a wedding.

At a little before six each day, little Willy would

position his sled in front of the old church on Main
Street. Today again he waited, eyes glued on the
big church clock that loomed high overhead.

Searchlight waited too—ears perked up, eyes
alert, legs slightly bent, ready to spring forward.

B-O-N-G!

At the first stroke of six, Searchlight lunged forward with such force that little Willy was almost
thrown from the sled. Straight down Main Street
they went, the sled's runners barely touching the
snow. They were one big blur as they turned right
onto North Road. And they were almost out of
town before the church clock became silent again.

"Go, Searchlight! Go!" Little Willy's voice sang
out across the snowy twilight. And did Searchlight
go! She had run this race a hundred times before,
and she knew the whereabouts of every fallen tree
and hidden gully. This enabled her to travel at
tremendous speed even though it was getting dark
and more dangerous.

Little Willy sucked in the cool night air and felt

the sting of the wind against his face. It was a race
all right. A race against time. A race against themselves. A race they always won.

The small building up ahead was Grandfather's
farmhouse. When Searchlight saw it, she seemed
to gather up every ounce of her remaining
strength. She forged ahead with such speed that
the sled seemed to lift up off the ground and fly.

· Searchlight ·

They were so exhausted when they arrived at
the house that neither of them noticed the horse
tied up outside.

Little Willy unhitched Searchlight, and then
both of them tumbled over onto their backs in the
snow and stared up at the moon. Searchlight had
her head and one paw on little Willy's chest and
was licking the underside of his chin. Little Willy
had a hold of Searchlight's ear, and he was grinning.

The owner of the horse stood on the front porch
and watched them, tapping his foot impatiently.

4

The Reason

"Get over here!" The voice cut through the air like the twang of a ricocheting bullet.

Little Willy had never heard a voice like that before. Not on this farm. He couldn't move.

But Searchlight sure could.

The owner of the voice barely had time to step back into the house and close the door.

Searchlight barked and snarled and jumped at the closed door. Then the door opened a crack. The man stood in the opening. He was holding a small derringer and pointing it at Searchlight. His hand was shaking.

"Don't shoot!" little Willy yelled as he reached out and touched Searchlight gently on the back. The barking stopped. "Who are you?"

"Name's Clifford Snyder. State of Wyoming," the man said with authority. He opened the door a little further.

The man was dressed as if he was going to a wedding. A city slicker. He was short, with a small head and a thin, droopy mustache that reminded little Willy of the last time he'd drunk a glass of milk in a hurry.

"What do you want?" little Willy asked.

"*Official* business. Can't the old man inside talk?"

"Not regular talk. We have a code. I can show you."

As little Willy reached for the door, Clifford Snyder again aimed his gun at Searchlight, who had begun to growl. "Leave that . . . *thing* outside," he demanded.

"She'll be all right if you put your gun away."

"No!"

"Are you afraid of her?"

"I'm not . . . afraid."

"Dogs can always tell when someone's afraid of them."

"Just get in this house this minute!" Clifford Snyder yelled, and his face turned red.

Little Willy left Searchlight outside. But Clifford Snyder wouldn't put his gun away until they were all the way into Grandfather's bedroom. And then he insisted that little Willy shut the door.

Grandfather's eyes were wide open and fixed on the ceiling. He looked much older and much more tired than he had this morning.

"You're no better than other folks," Clifford Snyder began as he lit up a long, thin cigar and blew smoke toward the ceiling. "And anyway, it's the law. Plain and simple."

Little Willy didn't say anything. He was busy combing Grandfather's hair, like he did every day when he got home. When he finished he held up

33

the mirror so Grandfather could see.

"I'm warning you," Clifford Snyder continued. "If you don't pay . . . we have our ways. And it's all legal. All fair and legal. You're no better than other folks."

"Do we owe you some money, Mr. Snyder?" little Willy asked.

"Taxes, son. Taxes on this farm. Your grandfather there hasn't been paying them."

Little Willy was confused.

Taxes? Grandfather had always paid every bill. And always on time. And little Willy did the same. So what was this about taxes? Grandfather had never mentioned them before. There must be some mistake.

"Is it true?" little Willy asked Grandfather.

But Grandfather didn't answer. Apparently he had gotten worse during the day. He didn't move his hand, or even his fingers.

"Ask him about the letters," piped up Clifford Snyder.

"What letters?"

"Every year we send a letter—a tax bill—showing how much you owe."

"I've never seen one," insisted little Willy.

"Probably threw 'em out."

"Are you sure . . ." began little Willy. And then he remembered the strongbox.

He removed the boards, then lifted the heavy box up onto the floor. He opened it and removed the papers. The papers he remembered seeing when he had looked for the money to rent the horse.

"Are these the letters?" he asked.

Clifford Snyder snatched the letters from little Willy's hand and examined them. "Yep, sure are," he said. "These go back over ten years." He held up one of the letters. "This here is the last one we sent."

Little Willy looked at the paper. There were so many figures and columns and numbers that he couldn't make any sense out of what he was looking at. "How much do we owe you, Mr. Snyder?"

"Says right here. Clear as a bell." The short man jabbed his short finger at the bottom of the page.

Little Willy's eyes popped open. "Five hundred dollars! We owe you five hundred dollars?"

Clifford Snyder nodded, rocking forward onto his toes, making himself taller. "And if you don't pay," he said, "I figure this here farm is just about worth—"

"You can't take our farm away!" little Willy screamed, and Searchlight began barking outside.

"Oh, yes, we can," Clifford Snyder said, smiling, exposing his yellow, tobacco-stained teeth.

5

The Way

The next day little Willy met the situation head on. Or, at least, he wanted to. But he wasn't sure just what to do.

Where was he going to get five hundred dollars?

Grandfather had always said, "Where there's a will, there's a way." Little Willy had the will. Now all he had to do was find the way.

"Of all the stupid things," cried Doc Smith. "Not paying his taxes. Let this be a lesson to you, Willy."

"But the potatoes barely bring in enough money

to live on," explained little Willy. "We went broke last year."

"Doesn't matter. Taxes gotta be paid, whether we like it or not. And believe me, I don't know of anybody who likes it."

"Then why do we have them in the first place?"

"Because it's the way the State gets its money."

"Why don't they grow potatoes like Grandfather does?"

Doc Smith laughed. "They have more important things to do than grow potatoes," she explained.

"Like what?"

"Like . . . taking care of us."

"Grandfather says we should take care of ourselves."

"But not all people *can* take care of themselves. Like the sick. Like your grandfather."

"I can take care of him. He took care of me when my mother died. Now I'm taking care of him."

"But what if something should happen to you?"

"Oh . . ." Little Willy thought about this.

They walked over to the sled, where Searchlight was waiting, Doc Smith's high boots sinking into the soft snow with each step.

Little Willy brushed the snow off Searchlight's back. Then he asked, "Owing all this money is the reason Grandfather got sick, isn't it?"

"I believe it is, Willy," she agreed.

"So if I pay the taxes, Grandfather will get better, won't he?"

Doc Smith rubbed the wrinkles below her eyes. "You just better do what I told you before, let Mrs. Peacock take care of your grandfather and—"

"But he will, he'll get better, won't he?"

"Yes, I'm sure he would. But, child, where are you going to get five hundred dollars?"

"I don't know. But I will. You'll see."

That afternoon little Willy stepped into the bank wearing his blue suit and his blue tie. His hair was so slicked down that it looked like wet paint. He asked to see Mr. Foster, the president of the bank.

Mr. Foster was a big man with a big cigar stuck right in the center of his big mouth. When he talked, the cigar bobbled up and down, and little Willy wondered why the ash didn't fall off the end of it.

Little Willy showed Mr. Foster the papers from Grandfather's strongbox and told him everything Clifford Snyder, the tax man, had said.

"Sell," Mr. Foster recommended after studying the papers. The cigar bobbled up and down. "Sell the farm and pay the taxes. If you don't, they can take the farm away from you. They have the right."

"I'll be eleven next year. I'll grow more potatoes than anybody's ever seen. You'll see . . ."

"You need five hundred dollars, Willy. Do you know how much that is? And anyway, there isn't enough time. Of course, the bank could loan you the money, but how could you pay it back? Then what about next year? No. I say sell before you end

up with nothing." The cigar ash fell onto the desk.
"I have fifty dollars in my savings account."

"I'm sorry, Willy," Mr. Foster said as he wiped
the ash off onto the floor.

As little Willy walked out of the bank with his
head down, Searchlight greeted him by placing
two muddy paws on his chest. Little Willy smiled
and grabbed Searchlight around the neck and
squeezed her as hard as he could. "We'll do it, girl.
You and me. We'll find the way."

The next day little Willy talked to everybody he
could think of. He talked with his teacher, Miss
Williams. He talked with Lester at the general
store. He even talked with Hank, who swept up
over at the post office.

They all agreed . . . sell the farm. That was the
only answer.

There was only one person left to talk to. If only
he could. "Should we sell?" little Willy asked.

Palm up meant "yes." Palm down meant "no."
Grandfather's hand lay motionless on the

42

bed. Searchlight barked. Grandfather's fingers twitched. But that was all.

Things looked hopeless.

And then little Willy found the way.

He was at Lester's General Store when it happened. When he saw the poster.

Every February the National Dogsled Races were held in Jackson, Wyoming. People came from all over to enter the race, and some of the finest dog teams in the country were represented. It was an open race—any number of dogs could be entered. Even one. The race covered ten miles of snow-covered countryside, starting and ending on Main Street right in front of the old church. There was a cash prize for the winner. The amount varied from year to year. This year it just happened to be five hundred dollars.

"Sure," Lester said as he pried the nail loose and handed little Willy the poster. "I'll pick up another at the mayor's office." Lester was skinny but strong, wore a white apron, and talked with saliva

on his lips. "Gonna be a good one this year. They say that mountain man, the Indian called Stone Fox, might come. Never lost a race. No wonder, with five Samoyeds."

But little Willy wasn't listening as he ran out of the store, clutching the poster in his hand. "Thank you, Lester. Thank you!"

Grandfather's eyes were fixed on the ceiling. Little Willy had to stand on his toes in order to position the poster directly in front of Grandfather's face.

"I'll win!" little Willy said. "You'll see. They'll never take this farm away."

Searchlight barked and put one paw up on the bed. Grandfather closed his eyes, squeezing out a tear that rolled down and filled up his ear. Little Willy gave Grandfather a big hug, and Searchlight barked again.

6

Stone Fox

Little Willy went to see Mayor Smiley at the city hall building in town to sign up for the race.

The mayor's office was large and smelled like hair tonic. The mayor sat in a bright red chair with his feet on his desk. There was nothing on the desk except the mayor's feet.

"We have a race for you youngsters one hour before." Mayor Smiley mopped sweat from his neck with a silk handkerchief, although little Willy thought it was quite cool in the room.

"I wanna enter the *real* race, Mr. Mayor."

"You must be funning, boy." The mayor

46

laughed twice and blotted his neck. "Anyway, there's an entrance fee."

"How much?"

"Fifty dollars."

Little Willy was stunned. That was a lot of money just to enter a race. But he was determined. He ran across the street to the bank.

"Don't be stupid," Mr. Foster told little Willy. "This is not a race for amateurs. Some of the best dog teams in the Northwest will be entering."

"I have Searchlight! We go fast as lightning. Really, Mr. Foster, we do."

Mr. Foster shook his head. "You don't stand a chance of winning."

"Yes, we do!"

"Willy . . . the money in your savings account is for your college education. You know I can't give it to you."

"You have to."

"I do?"

"It's *my* money!"

Little Willy left the bank with a stack of ten-dollar gold pieces—five of them, to be exact.

He walked into the mayor's office and plopped the coins down on the mayor's desk. "Me and Searchlight are gonna win that five hundred dollars, Mr. Mayor. You'll see. Everybody'll see."

Mayor Smiley counted the money, wiped his neck, and entered little Willy in the race.

When little Willy stepped out of the city hall building, he felt ten feet tall. He looked up and down the snow-covered street. He was grinning from ear to ear. Searchlight walked over and stood in front of the sled, waiting to be hitched up. But little Willy wasn't ready to go yet. He put his thumbs in his belt loops and let the sun warm his face.

He felt great. In his pocket was a map Mayor Smiley had given him showing the ten miles the race covered. Down Main Street, right on North Road—little Willy could hardly hold back his excitement.

Five miles of the race he traveled every day and knew with his eyes closed. The last five miles were back into town along South Road, which was mostly straight and flat. It's speed that would count here, and with the lead he knew he could get in the first five miles, little Willy was sure he could win.

As little Willy hitched Searchlight to the sled, something down at the end of the street—some moving objects—caught his eye. They were difficult to see because they were all white. There were five of them. And they were beautiful. In fact, they were the most beautiful Samoyeds little Willy had ever seen.

The dogs held their heads up proudly and strutted in unison. They pulled a large but lightly constructed sled. They also pulled a large—but by no means lightly constructed—man. Way down at the end of the street the man looked normal, but as the sled got closer, the man got bigger and bigger.

The man was an Indian—dressed in furs and leather, with moccasins that came all the way up to his knees. His skin was dark, his hair was dark, and he wore a dark-colored headband. His eyes sparkled in the sunlight, but the rest of his face was as hard as stone.

· *Stone Fox* ·

The sled came to a stop right next to little Willy. The boy's mouth hung open as he tilted his head way back to look up at the man. Little Willy had never seen a giant before.

"Gosh," little Willy gasped.

The Indian looked at little Willy. His face was solid granite, but his eyes were alive and cunning.

"Howdy," little Willy blurted out, and he gave a nervous smile.

But the Indian said nothing. His eyes shifted to Searchlight, who let out a soft moan but did not bark.

The Giant walked into the city hall building.

Word that Stone Fox had entered the race spread throughout the town of Jackson within the hour, and throughout the state of Wyoming within the day.

Stories and legends about the awesome mountain man followed shortly. Little Willy heard many of them at Lester's General Store.

51

· *Stone Fox* ·

"Was this time in Denver he snapped a man's back with two fingers," said Dusty, the town drunk. But nobody believed him, really.

Little Willy learned that no white man had ever heard Stone Fox talk. Stone Fox refused to speak with the white man because of the treatment his people had received. His tribe, the Shoshone, who were peaceful seed gatherers, had been forced to leave Utah and settle on a reservation in Wyoming with another tribe called the Arapaho.

Stone Fox's dream was for his people to return to their homeland. Stone Fox was using the money he won from racing to simply buy the land back. He had already purchased four farms and over two hundred acres.

That Stone Fox was smart, all right.

In the next week little Willy and Searchlight went over the ten-mile track every day, until they knew every inch of it by heart.

Stone Fox hardly practiced at all. In fact, little

STONE FOX

Willy only saw Stone Fox do the course once, and then he sure wasn't going very fast.

The race was scheduled for Saturday morning at ten o'clock. Only nine sleds were entered. Mayor Smiley had hoped for more contestants, but after Stone Fox had entered, well . . . you couldn't blame people for wanting to save their money.

It was true Stone Fox had never lost a race. But little Willy wasn't worried. He had made up his mind to win. And nothing was going to stop him. Not even Stone Fox.

7

The Meeting

It was Friday night, the night before the race, when it happened.

Grandfather was out of medicine. Little Willy went to see Doc Smith.

"Here." Doc Smith handed little Willy a piece of paper with some scribbling on it. "Take this to Lester right away."

"But it's nighttime. The store's closed."

"Just knock on the back door. He'll hear you."

"But . . . are you sure it's all right?"

"Yes. Lester knows I may have to call on him any time—day or night. People don't always get sick just during working hours, now, do they?"

"No, I guess they don't." Little Willy headed for the door. He sure wished he could stay and have some of that cinnamon cake Doc Smith was baking in the oven. It smelled mighty good. But Grandfather needed his medicine. And, anyway, he wouldn't think of staying without being asked.

"One other thing, Willy," Doc Smith said.

"Yes, ma'am?"

"I might as well say this now as later. It's about the race tomorrow."

"Yes, ma'am?"

"First, I want you to know that I think you're a darn fool for using your college money to enter that race."

Little Willy's eyes looked to the floor. "Yes, ma'am."

"But, since it's already been done, I also want you to know that I'll be rooting for you."

Little Willy looked up. "You will?"

"Win, Willy. Win that race tomorrow."

Little Willy beamed. He tried to speak, but couldn't find the words. Embarrassed, he backed over to the door, gave a little wave, then turned quickly to leave.

"And, Willy . . ."

"Yes, ma'am?"

"If you stay a minute, you can have some of that cinnamon cake I've got in the oven."

"Yes, ma'am!"

Later, on his way to town, little Willy sang at the top of his lungs. The sled's runners cut through the snow with a swish. This was a treacherous road at night, but the moon was out and Searchlight could see well. And, anyway, they knew this road by heart. Nothing was going to happen.

Lester gave little Willy a big bottle of what looked like dirty milk.

"How's your grandfather doing?" Lester asked.

"Not so good. But after I win the race tomorrow, he'll get better. Doc Smith thinks so too."

Lester smiled. "I admire you, Willy. You got

57

a heap of courage, going up against the likes of Stone Fox. You know he's never lost, don't you?"

"Yes, I know. Thank you for the medicine."

Little Willy waved good-bye as Searchlight started off down Main Street.

Lester watched the departing sled for a long time before he yelled, "Good luck, son!"

On his way out of town, along North Road, little Willy heard dogs barking. The sounds came from the old deserted barn near the schoolhouse.

Little Willy decided to investigate.

He squeaked open the barn door and peeked in. It was dark inside and he couldn't see anything. He couldn't hear anything either. The dogs had stopped barking.

He went inside the barn.

Little Willy's eyes took a while to get used to the dark, and then he saw them. The five Samoyeds. They were in the corner of the barn on a bed of straw. They were looking at him. They were so

beautiful that little Willy couldn't keep from smiling.

Little Willy loved dogs. He had to see the Samoyeds up close. They showed no alarm as he approached, or as he held out his hand to pet them.

And then it happened.

There was a movement through the darkness to little Willy's right. A sweeping motion, fast at first; then it appeared to slow and stop. But it didn't stop. A hand hit little Willy right in the face, sending him over backward.

"I didn't mean any harm, Mr. Stone Fox," little Willy said as he picked himself up off the ground, holding a hand over his eye.

Stone Fox stood tall in the darkness and said nothing. Searchlight barked outside. The Samoyeds barked in return.

Little Willy continued, "I'm going to race against you tomorrow. I know how you wanna win, but . . . I wanna win too. I gotta win. If I don't, they're gonna take away our farm. They have the right. Grandfather says that those that want to bad enough, will. So I will. I'll win. I'm gonna beat you."

Stone Fox remained motionless. And silent.

Little Willy backed over to the barn door, still holding his eye. "I'm sorry we both can't win," he said. Then he pushed open the barn door and left, closing the door behind him.

In the barn, Stone Fox stood unmoving for another moment; then he reached out with one massive hand and gently petted one of the Samoyeds.

That night little Willy couldn't sleep—his eye was killing him. And when little Willy couldn't sleep, Searchlight couldn't sleep. Both tossed and turned for hours, and whenever little Willy looked over to see if Searchlight was asleep, she'd just be lying there with her eyes wide open, staring back at him.

Little Willy needed his rest. So did Searchlight. Tomorrow was going to be a big day. The biggest day of their lives.

61

8

The Day

The day of the race arrived.

Little Willy got up early. He couldn't see out of his right eye. It was swollen shut.

As he fed Grandfather his oatmeal, he tried to hide his eye with his hand or by turning away, but he was sure Grandfather saw it just the same.

After adding more wood to the fire, little Willy kissed Grandfather, hitched up Searchlight, and started off for town.

At the edge of their property he stopped the sled for a moment and looked back at the farmhouse. The roof was covered with freshly fallen snow. A trail of smoke escaped from the stone chimney. The jagged peaks of the Teton Mountains shot up in the background toward the clear blue sky overhead. "Yes, sir," he remembered Grandfather saying. "There are some things in this world worth dying for."

Little Willy loved this country. He loved to hike and to fish and to camp out by a lake. But he did not like to hunt. He loved animals too much to be a hunter.

He had killed a bird once with a slingshot. But that had been when he was only six years old. And that had been enough. In fact, to this day, he still remembered the spot where the poor thing was buried.

Lost in his thoughts, little Willy got to town before he knew it. As he turned onto Main Street, he brought the sled to an abrupt halt.

He couldn't believe what he saw.

Main Street was jammed with people, lined up on both sides of the street. There were people on rooftops and people hanging out of windows. Little Willy hadn't expected such a big turnout. They must have all come to see Stone Fox.

Searchlight pulled the sled down Main Street past the crowd. Little Willy saw Miss Williams, his teacher, and Mr. Foster from the bank, and Hank from the post office. And there were Doc Smith and Mayor Smiley and Dusty the drunk. The city slickers were there. And even Clifford Snyder, the tax man, was there. Everybody.

Lester came out of the crowd and walked alongside little Willy for a while. It was one of the few times little Willy had ever seen Lester without his white apron.

"You can do it, Willy. You can beat him," Lester kept saying over and over again.

They had a race for the youngsters first, and the crowd cheered and rooted for their favorites. It was a short race. Just down to the end of Main Street and back. Little Willy didn't see who won. It didn't matter.

· *The Day* ·

And then it was time.

The old church clock showed a few minutes before ten as the contestants positioned themselves directly beneath the long banner that stretched across the street. They stood nine abreast. Stone Fox in the middle. Little Willy right next to him.

Little Willy had read all about the other contestants in the newspaper. They were all well-known mountain men with good racing records and excellent dog teams. But, even so, all bets were on Stone Fox. The odds were as high as a hundred to one that he'd win.

Not one cent had been bet on little Willy and Searchlight.

"What happened to Willy's eye?" Doc Smith asked Lester.

"Bumped it this morning when he got up, he told me. Just nervous. Got a right to be." Lester was chewing on his hand, his eyes glued on Stone Fox. "Big Indian," he whispered to himself.

Although little Willy's eye was black, puffy, and

swollen shut, he still felt like a winner. He was smiling. Searchlight knew the route as well as he did, so it really didn't matter if he could see at all. They were going to win today, and that was final. Both of them knew it.

Stone Fox looked bigger than ever standing next to little Willy. In fact, the top of little Willy's head was dead even with Stone Fox's waist.

"Morning, Mr. Stone Fox," little Willy said, looking practically straight up. "Sure's a nice day for a race."

Stone Fox must have heard little Willy, but he did not look at him. His face was frozen like ice, and his eyes seemed to lack that sparkle little Willy remembered seeing before.

The crowd became silent as Mayor Smiley stepped out into the street.

Miss Williams clenched her hands together until her knuckles turned white. Lester's mouth hung open, his lips wet. Mr. Foster began chewing his cigar. Hank stared without blinking. Doc Smith

67

held her head up proudly. Dusty took a powerful swig from a whiskey bottle. Clifford Snyder removed a gold watch from his vest pocket and checked the time.

Tension filled the air.

Little Willy's throat became dry. His hands started to sweat. He could feel his heart thumping.

Mayor Smiley raised a pistol to the sky and fired.

The race had begun!

9

The Race

Searchlight sprang forward with such force that little Willy couldn't hang on. If it weren't for a lucky grab, he would have fallen off the sled for sure.

In what seemed only seconds, little Willy and Searchlight had traveled down Main Street, turned onto North Road, and were gone. Far, far ahead of the others. They were winning. At least for the moment.

Stone Fox started off dead last. He went so slowly down Main Street that everyone was sure something must be wrong.

Swish! Little Willy's sled flew by the school-house on the outskirts of town, and then by the old deserted barn.

Swish! Swish! Swish! Other racers followed in hot pursuit.

"Go, Searchlight! Go!" little Willy sang out. The cold wind pressed against his face, causing his good eye to shut almost completely. The snow was well packed. It was going to be a fast race today. The fastest they had ever run.

The road was full of dangerous twists and turns, but little Willy did not have to slow down as the other racers did. With only one dog and a small sled, he was able to take the sharp turns at full speed without risk of sliding off the road or losing control.

Therefore, with each turn, little Willy pulled farther and farther ahead.

Swish! The sled rounded a corner, sending snow flying. Little Willy was smiling. This was fun!

About three miles out of town the road made a

half circle around a frozen lake. Instead of following the turn, little Willy took a shortcut right across the lake. This was tricky going, but Searchlight had done it many times before.

Little Willy had asked Mayor Smiley if he was permitted to go across the lake, not wanting to be disqualified. "As long as you leave town heading north and come back on South Road," the mayor had said, "anything goes!"

None of the other racers attempted to cross the lake. Not even Stone Fox. The risk of falling through the ice was just too great.

Little Willy's lead increased.

Stone Fox was still running in last place. But he was picking up speed.

At the end of five miles, little Willy was so far out in front that he couldn't see anybody behind him when he looked back.

He knew, however, that the return five miles, going back into town, would not be this easy. The trail along South Road was practically straight and very smooth, and Stone Fox was sure to close the gap. But by how much? Little Willy didn't know.

Doc Smith's house flew by on the right. The tall trees surrounding her cabin seemed like one solid wall.

Grandfather's farm was coming up next.

When Searchlight saw the farmhouse, she started to pick up speed. "No, girl," little Willy yelled. "Not yet."

As they approached the farmhouse, little Willy thought he saw someone in Grandfather's bedroom window. It was difficult to see with only one good eye. The someone was a man. With a full beard.

It couldn't be. But it was! It was Grandfather!

Grandfather was sitting up in bed. He was looking out the window.

Little Willy was so excited he couldn't think straight. He started to stop the sled, but Grandfather indicated no, waving him on. "Of course," little Willy said to himself. "I must finish the race. I haven't won yet."

"Go, Searchlight!" little Willy shrieked. "Go, girl!"

Grandfather was better. Tears of joy rolled down little Willy's smiling face. Everything was going to be all right.

And then Stone Fox made his move.

One by one he began to pass the other racers. He went from last place to eighth. Then from eighth place to seventh. Then from seventh to sixth. Sixth to fifth.

He passed the others as if they were standing still.

He went from fifth place to fourth. Then to third. Then to second.

Until only little Willy remained.

But little Willy still had a good lead. In fact, it was not until the last two miles of the race that Stone Fox got his first glimpse of little Willy since the race had begun.

The five Samoyeds looked magnificent as they

moved effortlessly across the snow. Stone Fox was gaining, and he was gaining fast. And little Willy wasn't aware of it.

Look back, little Willy! Look back!

But little Willy didn't look back. He was busy thinking about Grandfather. He could hear him laughing . . . and playing his harmonica . . .

Finally little Willy glanced back over his shoulder. He couldn't believe what he saw! Stone Fox was nearly on top of him!

This made little Willy mad. Mad at himself. Why hadn't he looked back more often? What was he doing? He hadn't won yet. Well, no time to think of that now. He had a race to win.

"Go, Searchlight! Go, girl!"

But Stone Fox kept gaining. Silently. Steadily.

"Go, Searchlight! Go!"

The lead Samoyed passed little Willy and pulled up even with Searchlight. Then it was a nose ahead. But that was all. Searchlight moved forward, inching *her* nose ahead. Then the Samoyed

regained the lead. Then Searchlight . . .

When you enter the town of Jackson on South Road, the first buildings come into view about a half a mile away. Whether Searchlight took those buildings to be Grandfather's farmhouse again, no one can be sure, but it was at this time that she poured on the steam.

Little Willy's sled seemed to lift up off the ground and fly. Stone Fox was left behind.

But not that far behind.

10

The Finish Line

The crowd cheered madly when they saw little Willy come into view at the far end of Main Street, and even more madly when they saw that Stone Fox was right on his tail.

"Go, Searchlight! Go!"

Searchlight forged ahead. But Stone Fox was gaining!

"Go, Searchlight! Go!" little Willy cried out.

Searchlight gave it everything she had.

She was a hundred feet from the finish line when her heart burst. She died instantly. There was no suffering.

The sled and little Willy tumbled over her, slid along the snow for a while, then came to a stop about ten feet from the finish line. It had started to snow—white snowflakes landed on Searchlight's dark fur as she lay motionless on the ground.

The crowd became deathly silent.

Lester's eyes looked to the ground. Miss Williams had her hands over her mouth. Mr. Foster's cigar lay on the snow. Doc Smith started to run out to little Willy, but stopped. Mayor Smiley looked shocked and helpless. And so did Hank and Dusty, and so did the city slickers, and so did Clifford Snyder, the tax man.

Stone Fox brought his sled to a stop alongside little Willy. He stood tall in the icy wind and looked down at the young challenger, and at the dog that lay limp in his arms.

"Is she dead, Mr. Stone Fox? Is she dead?" little Willy asked, looking up at Stone Fox with his one good eye.

Stone Fox knelt down and put one massive hand

on Searchlight's chest. He felt no heartbeat. He looked at little Willy, and the boy understood.

Little Willy squeezed Searchlight with all his might. "You did real good, girl. Real good. I'm real proud of you. You rest now. Just rest." Little Willy began to brush the snow off Searchlight's back.

Stone Fox stood up slowly.

No one spoke. No one moved. All eyes were on the Indian, the one called Stone Fox, the one who had never lost a race, and who now had another victory within his grasp.

But Stone Fox did nothing.

He just stood there. Like a mountain.

His eyes shifted to his own dogs, then to the finish line, then back to little Willy, holding Searchlight.

With the heel of his moccasin Stone Fox drew a long line in the snow. Then he walked back over to his sled and pulled out his rifle.

Down at the end of Main Street, the other racers

began to appear. As they approached, Stone Fox fired his rifle into the air. They came to a stop.

Stone Fox spoke.

"Anyone crosses this line—I shoot."

And there wasn't anybody who didn't believe him.

Stone Fox nodded to the boy.

The town looked on in silence as little Willy, carrying Searchlight, walked the last ten feet and across the finish line.

The idea for this story came from a Rocky Mountain legend that was told to me in 1974 by Bob Hudson over a cup of coffee at Hudson's Café in Idaho Falls, Idaho. Although Stone Fox and the other characters are purely fictitious and of my creation, the tragic ending to this story belongs to the legend and is reported to have actually happened.

RACE DAYS

by Sallie Luther

The sled dogs are ready. The clock is counting down. Soon the races will begin!

How do you like to race — on foot, on your bike, on a fast pony? Kids in snowy places such as Alaska have another favorite way. They race sleds pulled by dogs. These kids often have parents who race sled dogs too.

People who use sleds pulled by dogs are called *mushers*. In long-ago days, mushers used teams of dogs to pull sleds packed with supplies. The mushers and their teams could skim across ice and snow into places where horses, boats, or trucks couldn't go.

Dog teams don't haul stuff around much anymore. But teams of *racing* dogs are popping up all over Alaska.

Racing teams don't have to be made up of any special *breed* (kind) of dog. Huskies, such as the dog on the left, are a favorite for racing teams. But other dogs are used too, such as the larger, heavier husky look-alikes called malamutes (MAH-luh-mutes). And you might be surprised to find out that even poodles sometimes pull sleds.

But whatever their breed, sled dogs must be tough and strong. And most of all, they must like to *race*.

Get Ready

When race day comes, it's hard to tell who's more excited — the mushers or their dogs. They've all been getting ready for such a long time.

Lots of kids raise and train their own sled dogs. And they

make sure the dogs are well fed and cared for in other ways while being trained. The dogs have to be healthy and happy to race well.

The youngest kids have just one or two dogs pulling their sleds. But older kids use teams of three or more dogs. They train the team to work together and follow the lead dog. This dog runs first in line and is often the fastest dog.

How do the dogs know where to go? The musher has trained the lead dog to follow commands. When a musher calls "Hike," or "All right," the lead dog starts running. It learns other words too. The musher might shout "Gee" or "Haw." These commands mean "turn right" or "turn left." And a really important command is "Whoa!" which means "stop."

Besides training their dogs, mushers have to get their sleds in tip-top shape for race day:

The *basket*, or body of the sled, rides on *runners*. These stick out far enough behind the basket for the musher to stand on. A *brake* slows or stops the sled whenever the musher steps on it. *Harnesses* and *tug lines* hitch the dogs to a main *tow line*. This line is what the dogs pull to make the sled race along.

Get Set

Race day is here! Dogs whine and wiggle. Kids laugh and talk with friends while waiting for their turn to race. The air is frosty cold, but the kids hardly notice — they're bundled up so well.

It's February in Alaska, and that means it's time for the Anchorage Fur Rendezvous (RON-day-voo) Alascom Junior World Championship. But who can remember a long, complicated name like that? So the kids call their races the "Fur Rondy" for short.

There are lots of different races in the Fur Rondy. The very youngest mushers start out by racing for about two miles (3.2 km). As they grow older, they race farther.

The mushers don't start to race at the same time. Instead, they leave the starting line about two minutes apart.

The races are held for three days. Each musher must run three races — one on each day — to finish. A score-keeper adds up how long it takes each musher to run all three races. And the mushers with the lowest totals are the winners.

All right — the first races are about to begin. Pretend for a moment that the starter has called your number, and it's your turn to race.

You and your dogs move up to the starting line. Now the final countdown begins:

Ten . . . nine . . . eight . . . *(Your dogs know what's coming and prance eagerly.)* Seven . . . six . . . five . . . *(You take a deep breath and get a good grip on your sled.)* Four . . . three . . . two . . . one . . .

Go!

"Hike, hike, *hike!*" you yell. Your dogs dig in and yank the sled into motion. You remind yourself not to let go — no matter what.

Now you're swishing along down a snowy track. Tiny ice crystals sting your face as they're kicked up by your dogs. For a blazing-fast few minutes, it's easy to believe that you and your dogs are alone in the wilderness.

Suddenly you see curves ahead. "Gee!" you shout, then, "Haw!" as the dogs swing first right, then left. You shift your weight to help guide the sled.

You push with one foot for an extra power boost going uphill. You step on the brake to slow the sled and steady it as you rush downhill.

Then you hit the home stretch. You take a deep breath and urge your dogs to run faster: "C'mon, c'mon, *move it!*" And they give you everything they've got as you flash across the finish line.

You didn't have the fastest time today, but there are two more races before the championship is decided. And there's always next year!

Later you bring your dogs into their cozy trailer. They'll get a good meal, a good rest, and loads of hugs from their proud musher.

Mighty Mushing Machine

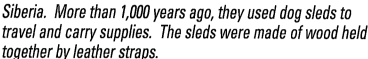

The first dog sledders were the natives of North America and Siberia. More than 1,000 years ago, they used dog sleds to travel and carry supplies. The sleds were made of wood held together by leather straps.

Today's sleds look much like those ancient sleds, but there are some important differences. Here's what today's dog sledders are using:

THE SLED

The sled is made of wood from ash or birch trees. It slides over the snow on *runners*, and is steered from the back with a handlebar or *driving bow*.

SNOW HOOK

This holds the sled and dogs in place during stops.

THE EQUIPMENT OR DOG BAG

The equipment or dog bag carries clothing, tools, or supplies. It can also carry an injured or tired dog during a race.

THE BRAKE

The brake is attached to the back of the sled. When the musher pushes it down with a foot, it drags in the snow and stops the sled.

SLED DOGS

The Samoyed (pictured here), Alaskan Malamute, Siberian Husky, and Alaskan Husky are dogs most often used in races. A harness attached to a hitch line connects the dogs to the sled.

The Iditarod Trail Sled Dog Race

The Iditarod Trail Sled Dog Race is named after an old gold-mining town in Alaska. In 1925, an epidemic of diphtheria broke out in Nome. Without the proper medicine, many people's lives were in danger. The only way to get the medicine to Nome was by dog sled along the old trail that had connected the mining town of Iditarod to Anchorage — a treacherous trail that had hardly been used in nearly twenty years.

Volunteer mushers carried the serum to Nome in record time, ending the epidemic. The mushers and their dogs became national heroes.

The Iditarod Trail Sled Dog Race is a tribute to that rough, winding trail and the men and women who made it famous.

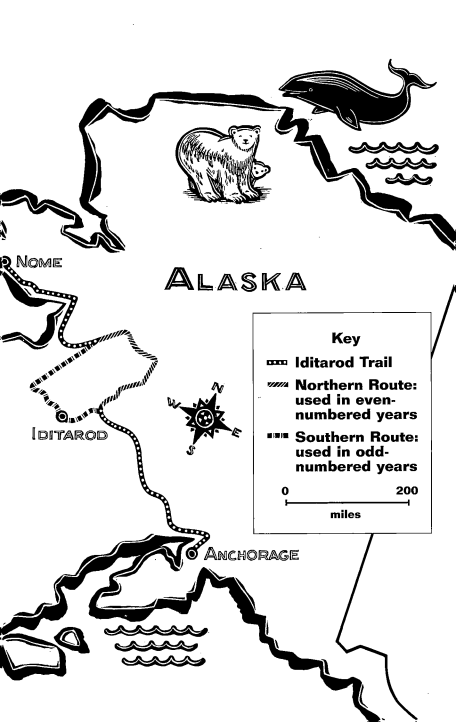

NOME

ALASKA

IDITAROD

ANCHORAGE

Key

▪▪▪ **Iditarod Trail**

▨▨ **Northern Route: used in even-numbered years**

◼▮◼ **Southern Route: used in odd-numbered years**

0   200

miles

N
W   E
S

A Doggone Champion:
Susan Butcher

by Layne Cameron

Susan Butcher sped across the frozen bay on her sled. Suddenly, all thoughts of winning the race were thrown aside by a horrifying sound. The ice was breaking up! Before she could make it across the bay, the ice shattered under her feet. Susan and her sled plunged into the dark, icy waters.

Granite, the lead dog, acted fast. He urged the dog team to pull with all its strength. Grunting with effort, their feet slipping on the ice, the dogs pulled Susan and the sled out of the freezing water. The team had saved her life!

Susan eventually thawed out — and still managed to finish in second place.

Susan Butcher is a champion's champion. She has won the grueling 1,049-mile Iditarod Trail Sled Dog Race four times!

Protecting Your Friends

During the next year's Iditarod, it was the dogs — not Susan — who fell into danger. Susan was speeding along, leading many other racers. Suddenly, she and her team ran across a moose on the trail.

Moose are huge animals. Adults can stand over six feet tall at the shoulder and weigh more than 1,500 pounds! This moose was starving. It became very angry and viciously attacked the dog team. Susan tried everything to scare it away — yelling at it and hitting it — but nothing worked.

The moose was wild! It rampaged for twenty minutes, stomping and tearing. Finally, someone had to shoot the moose before it did any more damage. In the end, two of Susan's dogs were killed and eleven others were injured.

She dropped out of the race and traveled with them to the veterinary hospital. Susan slept on the floor and stayed until the dogs were healthy.

"That was a tough year," she admits. "It was tough to come home and see two of my friends' houses empty."

After this tragedy, Susan worked even harder. She won the next three Iditarods. She is the only person ever to win three Iditarod races in a row!

"There are many hard things in life, but there is only one sad thing," Susan explains, "and that is giving up."

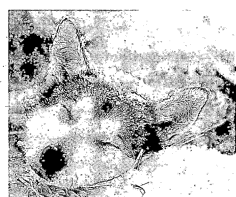

When your fur is as thick as Tuffy's, you can sleep just about anywhere — even in a snowstorm!

Born to Mush

Susan has loved animals since she was a kid. In Cambridge, Massachusetts, she often took care of her school's pets on the weekends.

"My mom would have iguanas crawling up her curtains," she says, laughing.

At age sixteen, Susan received a Siberian Husky. Huskies are bred to be sled dogs. To learn more about her dog, she read books and traveled to local sled dog events.

Soon Susan decided to become a musher. A musher is someone who races sled dogs. She got another dog and moved to Colorado. There she studied veterinary medicine while working at a dog-racing kennel.

Finally, after reading an article about the great Iditarod sled race, she decided she wanted to move to Alaska. The harsh weather and tough terrain appealed to her sense of adventure.

Iditarod or Bust

Sometimes Susan goes for months without seeing another person. But she isn't lonely. Susan has her dogs to keep her company. Together they train like professional athletes in the wilderness of Alaska.

She keeps close track of the dogs' diet, endurance, and overall health. Susan also listens to her dogs "talk." From their barks and howls, she knows if they are happy or sad, if someone is coming — even if the weather is going to change! "To understand them, you must know how they act and what signals they are sending you," she explains. Very few mushers have this close a relationship with their dogs.

Susan trusts her dogs. Their instincts have saved her life more than once — and have helped her become the doggone champion that she is today!

Above left: The Iditarod Trail leads Susan directly across a lake — frozen solid, slick as glass, and cold, cold, cold. Bottom left: Susan on the Iditarod Trail

Dog Heroes

*D*uring a diphtheria outbreak in Alaska in 1925, Togo led a sled-dog team to carry medicine from Anchorage to Nome. Togo led for 260 miles, almost five times farther than any of the other lead dogs!

*T*ravis Stout and his dog Kosmic work together to give Travis freedom that he could not have alone.

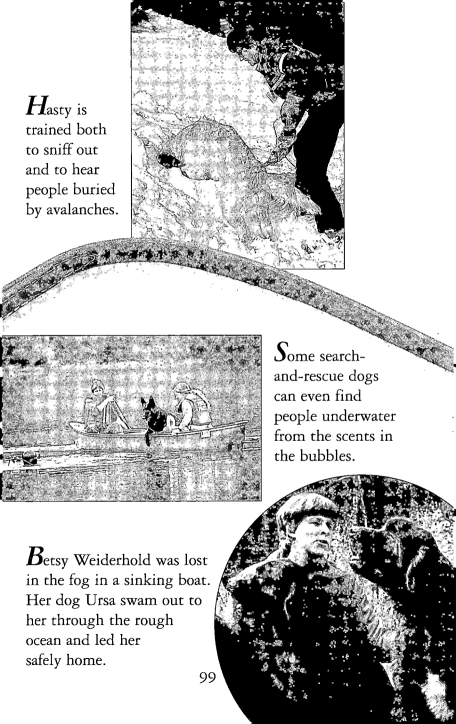

*H*asty is trained both to sniff out and to hear people buried by avalanches.

*S*ome search-and-rescue dogs can even find people underwater from the scents in the bubbles.

*B*etsy Weiderhold was lost in the fog in a sinking boat. Her dog Ursa swam out to her through the rough ocean and led her safely home.

99

Good Sledding

Ed Moody:
Master Dog Sled Builder

"Good Sledding, Ed Moody." That signature tells you the dog sled you're riding was made by master dog sled builder, Ed Moody.

Ed Moody was one of the first commercial dog sled builders in the United States. "It must have been seventy-two years ago, I built my first sled," says Ed. "I was twelve years old. It didn't look like the ones I make now, of course. But each year the sleds got a little better."

Now Ed Moody is a legend among sled builders. Mushers from all over the world call to order Moody sleds. It's been said that if you lined up end-to-end all the dog sleds he's made, they would stretch from Boston to Montreal. That's a whole lot of dog sleds!

To build a dog sled, Ed starts with a tree. He's been known to cut down a tree, saw it into boards, then make the different sled parts in his small workshop in Rochester, New Hampshire. Once the parts are made, Ed can assemble a sled in less than a day.

Dog sledding has been a life-long love for Ed Moody. He started dog sledding in New Hampshire as a boy. When he was twenty-two, he was along on Admiral Richard Byrd's historic expeditions to Antarctica in the 1930s. Ed was in charge of the expedition's dog sled teams.

Ed Moody on a 1933 expedition, outfitted for the cold climate of Antarctica

Far left: Ed Moody today, working in his shop and with a completed sled

At eighty-three, Ed is still building sleds and passing on his knowledge to his daughter, Roz, and his apprentice, Jeff. Ed thinks that not enough dog sled racers and builders have shared their knowledge. But he wants to pass on the tradition. "You can't say that I haven't left something behind," says the sled building master.

Good Sledding
Ed. Moody

A young Ed Moody with a pup during a trip to Antarctica in 1935

Below: A recent photo of Ed Moody with a new friend. He has loved the hardy sled dogs all his life.

102